Your Gift!

As a way of saying thanks for your purchase, we are offering an exclusive gift for readers of this book — our electronic tutorial:

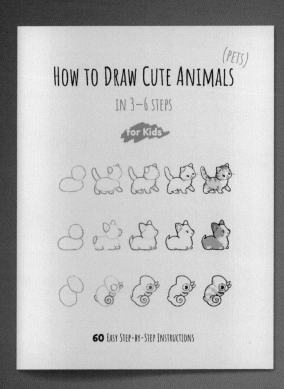

Get it at the link:

https://cutt.ly/UTSkUCz

Or use QR-Code:

Contents

Ellie Meyer

Five-Minute Bedtime Sleepy Stories

Illusratered by

Yaroslava Myroshnychenko

Maya and the Dream Dragon

Darkness blanketed the city. One by one, the children's bedroom lights went out, and, one by one, the stars in the night sky flickered on. This was the time, Maya knew, when the dream dragons came.

Tucked between the soft quilts of her bed, Maya was as cozy as could be. But she was not sleepy at all. A thousand fanciful dreams danced around in her head, and she couldn't decide which to choose. So when, just outside her window, the flash of moonlit scales caught her eye, she wrapped a quilt about her and tiptoed across the floor.

Raising her window to lean outside, she saw, floating only inches away, the enormous, scaly head of a dream dragon. Its long, snake-like body floated on the night's breeze, shimmering from blue, to black, to moonlight white.

"Shouldn't you be readying to dream, Little Girl?" asked the dragon in surprise.

"I can't," replied Maya. "I have too many dreams. I can't decide which to choose."

"Ahhhh," said the dream dragon, its big, dinner-plate eyes shining like starlight. "Then maybe you can help me. Many children still do not have a dream for tonight."

Carefully, Maya climbed out the window, clinging to the horns on the dragon's broad, scaly head. "Hold on tightly," said the dragon, and away they sailed.

Back and forth, in and out among the tall apartment buildings they weaved. Here and there the dragon would stop, floating on the night breeze just before the window of a sleeping child.

"I bet she'd like a dream about fairies," suggested Maya, "the kind that sleep with the bees in flowers." And the dragon breathed the dream, fairies, bees, flowers, and all, through the window into the bedroom.

One by one, Maya told her dreams to the dream dragon, and he gently exhaled them into the sleepy heads of children across the city.

The dragon then soared over snowy mountain peaks to mountain towns, where Maya left dreams of the sea and of the animals that lived beneath the waves. He sailed from cabin to cabin in wooded valleys, where she left dreams of skyscrapers, stadiums, and great city lights.

When every child at last had a dream to dream, the dragon returned Maya to her own window in the city. "And what dream did you keep for yourself" he asked, as Maya crawled down his big, scaly nose and back through her bedroom window.

Maya smiled and looked directly into the dragon's shining, dinner-plate eye. "A dream of a very special dragon," she said.

Owlet Goes Out

Dusk was falling over the wood, and Mother Owl was getting ready to fly. She gave Owlet a kiss on the fluff of his head. "I'll be back soon," she cooed. "Remember to stay right here, safe in the tree."

"I will," replied Owlet, as Mother Owl spread her wings and swooped off into the night.

Owlet perched in the hole in the tree that served as his window to the world. The landscape below him was lit by moonlight. The night creatures were all busied themselves, and the forest was alive with sounds.

One very curious sound captured Owlet's attention. It came from just below the tree hole.

"Good night! Good night!" it chirruped.

"I wonder," thought Owlet, "What could it be?" With wobbly little steps he climbed down from the edge of the tree hole to a branch just below. A shiny, black-brown cricket was chirruping. "Good night! Good night! Good night!" it said.

Just then a bat swooped down and blew by Owlet to catch a juicy gnat for dinner. Owlet gave a hoot of startled surprise. His little legs wobbled on the branch. His little wings fluttered as he tried to find his balance. But it was too late.

Down,

down,

down he tumbled, all the way to the leafy forest floor below.

"Oh, dear," he cried, looking up at the tree hole so far above his head. "How will I ever get home?"

The bat had swooped down again to help. "Climb up to that tree stump," it suggested, "and take a deep breath."

"Spread your wings," said a flying squirrel, "and hop up and down."

"Sing, 'Up and away! Up and away!'" chirruped the cricket.

"Think light, like a feather," hummed a glowing firefly.

"Wait for a nice, gentle breeze," advised a spindly spider swaying from its web.

Owlet scrambled to the top of a tree stump. He took a deep breath. He spread his wings and hopped up and down. "Up and away! Up and away," he sang. He thought light, like a feather, and waited for a gentle, passing breeze. Before he even knew it, Owlet was flying.

"Hooray!" cried the animals.

"Thank you!" hooted Owlet, as he flew up, up, up, to his hole in the tree above.

There Mother Owl waited anxiously for her little owlet. When she saw him flying, she hooted with delight. "Tomorrow night," cooed she, planting another kiss on his fluffy little head, "We two will fly out together."

Mera and the Lightening Bug

In the enchanted forest on Dream Mountain lived a community of small magic-folk that rode lightning bugs through the night sky. The firefly folk—or so they were called—slept during the day and arose with the setting sun. Then, in the hundreds of thousands, they mounted their nickering, flickering bugs and, grasping the edges of dusk, drew the blanket of night over all the forest, singing as they went:

Good night, good night, dear creatures of Dream Mountain!
Sleep tight, rest well, 'neath the dreamy light of Moon.
Good night, sleep tight, bird and beast, tree and fountain;
the morrow, sweet morrow, will welcome you soon.

All but little Mera, that is, who was the very smallest of the magic folk—too small, even, to ride a firefly.

And so it was that, night after night, Mera watched from the flower beds as her people mounted their lightning bugs and flew off in song. And so it was, too, that, night after night, she curled up in her flower and cried, and cried, and cried.

On one particularly lonely night, night, Mera cried out in her frustration, "Why should I be so neglected and forgotten, and all because of my size?" cried she. "I am brave. I am strong. And I know by heart The Song of the Dusk Ride."

At her words, a humming-buzzing sound drew near to Mera's flower. "Who is that?" a voice demanded.

"It is I, little Mera," she replied, peeking out of her flower to discover the largest lightning bug she had ever seen. Its colors were grayed with age. Its ancient wings were thin as paper. Its lightning flicker was dim and dying. But it spoke with a proud and mighty voice.

"I, too, know the Song of the Dusk Ride, little one. But the riders I carried are now too heavy for my old wings. They seek wild, young fireflies for the ride. I, too, have been forgotten." The firefly looked into the surprised face of Mera, the littlest of the firefly folk. "But you are so—so very small."

"I am," said Mera, standing to her feet to look as large as possible, "the very smallest. But I am brave. And strong."

The grandfather firefly smiled—as a firefly smiles—and nodded. "I would be honored to take you to where the dusk begins."

And so it was that Mera climbed up onto the back of the greatest and oldest of the fireflies on Dream Mountain. And, together, they joined the others in pulling in the cover of night, their voices singing bravely, strongly, with the rest:

Good night, good night, dear creatures of Dream Mountain!
Sleep tight, rest well, 'neath the dreamy light of Moon.
Good night, sleep tight, bird and beast, tree and fountain;
the morrow, sweet morrow, will welcome you soon.

The Not-So-Sleepy Princess

The sun was setting over the Kingdom of Dreams as, one by one, the citizens of the kingdom were tucking themselves into bed. Everyone, that is, except the little princess. She was not at all sleepy. No, not a bit!

The king and queen were frantic. Whatever could they do to get her to bed?

The king rubbed his nose. "Hmmmm..." he said aloud. "A lullaby is just what my little princess needs." So he awoke his very best minstrel.

The minstrel strummed his little wooden lute and hummed a sleepy, dreamy little song. But the little princess, her face lit with sheer delight, jumped up in her bed and began to clap and dance.

"Oh, my!" said the king.

"Don't worry; I know just the thing!" assured the queen, calling the cook from her berth in the kitchen. "A cup of warm, sweet milk will do the trick."

But in one great gulp the little princess drank down the warm, sweet milk. She burped one delicate, little princess burp and asked, "More, please!"

The king pulled his beard. "Hmmmm..." he said. "A good pillow-fluffing is the best bedtime trick." So he awoke the chambermaids, who fluff-fluff-fluffed every pillow on the princess's fluffy little princess bed.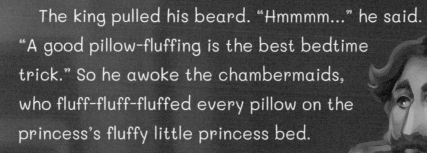

The little princess giggled. Tossing the pillows into the air, she wanted to fluff-fluff-fluff them too.

The king and queen sighed and scratched their heads. Then, one after another, they awoke everyone in the kingdom to help their not-so-sleepy princess.

They called in the seamstress to stitch soft, fleecy new pajamas.

They called in the mummers to read her a bedtime story.

They called in the jester to tell long, boring, bedtime jokes.

They called in the shepherd—and his sheep—that she might count them all.

And they called in even the magician, in hopes that he would cast a sleeping spell.

And all to no avail. Still, the princess was not sleepy. Not a bit!

Now it was late. The sun had set many hours ago. And, still, the princess was bubbling with glee.

The king and queen were oh, so tired. In the midst of the minstrel, magician, and mummers, the jesters and their jokes, and the seamstress, shepherds, and sheep, they finally sat down upon their little daughter's fluffy, princess bed and fell fast asleep.

At this, the little princess smiled. She bent over her parents' faces and gave them each a little kiss, then curled up right between the two, closing her eyes at long, long last.

Then, with collective sigh of relief, all in the Kingdom of Dreams returned to their homes and tucked themselves back into bed for a good night's sleep.

The Cat's Pajamas

The Mouse family lived in a big old house in a modest little hole in the wall. Winter was coming, and its cold weather, too. So, late one night, Papa Mouse made an announcement to his family.

"This winter," he declared, "we will not be as cold as the last. Tonight, we will have ourselves some new, cozy, fleecy-warm pajamas!"

"Hooray!" cheered the Mouse family.

"But where will we get the cloth?" asked Mama Mouse.

"Why, from our dear old Furball," answered Papa Mouse.

"Oh, no!" cried Mama.

Furball was the enormous, mean, old cat that shared the house. The cat had a nice, new set of cozy, fleecy-warm pajamas.

"Oh, yes," insisted Papa Mouse. "After all, with such a great fluff of fur, that fat old feline certainly has not need of pajamas!"

So, off crept most of the Mouse family, through the dark, chill night of the big, old house, off to find the cat—and his pajamas.

Furball was lying belly-up by the kitchen furnace. His fishy cat breath rumbled in and out. His long, white whiskers floated up and down. His gigantic pink paws twitched every now and again, showing his very long, very sharp and dangerous claws.

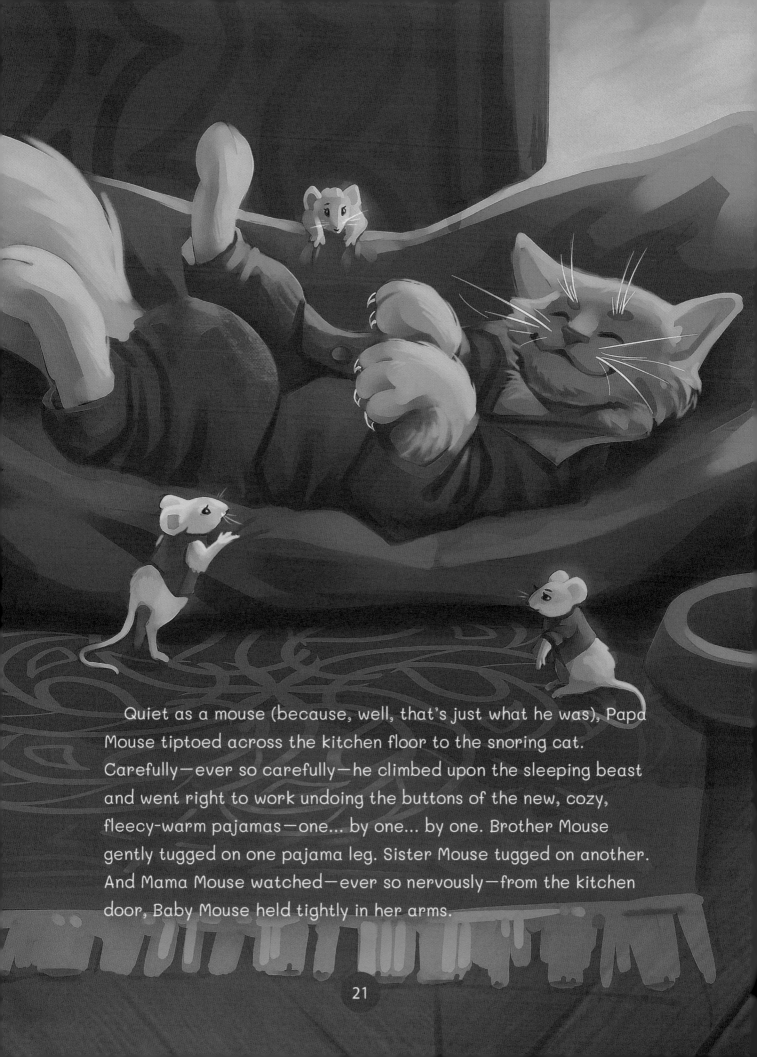

Quiet as a mouse (because, well, that's just what he was), Papa Mouse tiptoed across the kitchen floor to the snoring cat. Carefully—ever so carefully—he climbed upon the sleeping beast and went right to work undoing the buttons of the new, cozy, fleecy-warm pajamas—one... by one... by one. Brother Mouse gently tugged on one pajama leg. Sister Mouse tugged on another. And Mama Mouse watched—ever so nervously—from the kitchen door, Baby Mouse held tightly in her arms.

Just then, POP! The last button let go and went flying up, up into the air. The Mouse family gasped and held onto their breaths.

Clonk! Clink! Rivvely, rivvely, rivvely, rivelly... plat!

The button bounced and rolled, then finally fell flat. Furball opened his big toothy mouth and let out a long, lion-like yawn. He stretched his fat legs, licked his long, long whiskers—and went promptly back to sleep.

Then gently—every so gently—the mice tugged again and again, the first leg and then the second, the third and then the fourth, a little more and a little more, until finally the pajamas came free.

They raced then, back through the big, old house to their modest little hole in the wall, cat's pajamas held high in delight.

"Tonight," smiled Mama Mouse, taking out her needle and thread, "new, cozy, fleecy-warm pajamas for everyone!"

Hoshi the Starherd

The sun had ducked beneath the horizon, and dusk was darkening to night. The first stars would appear at any moment.

"Are you ready, Hoshi?" called his father from the door of their moon hut.

"Of course he's ready," smiled his mother. And ready Hoshi was. He was already washed and dressed, in fact, his newly-carved starherd staff in hand.

Hoshi waved goodbye to his mother, and walked along with his father to the edge of the moon. Then, they stepped off into the sky on their way to herd the stars. "Why do we herd the stars, son?" Hoshi's father asked, as a teacher asks his student before a test.

"So that people have stories to tell one another when they look into the skies at night."

"Very good," nodded Hoshi's father.

"Can I create any story I want?" asked Hoshi, "Like one about a fire-breathing dragon?"

"Draw from your heart, dear son," said his father. "And listen to the stars. They will help you find the right story to tell." And off he went, to herd the farthest stars while Hoshi stayed nearer to home.

As a king plants his scepter firmly on the tiles of his court, Hoshi drove his staff against the ground. He cleared his throat and commanded the stars, "I am Hoshi the starherd. Tonight you will make for me a fire-breathing dragon!"

But the stars around him only blinked and began to wander away.

With his hook, Hoshi prodded and pushed and pulled them. He tried to put them in a line. Or form them in an arc. Or make them stay—at the very least—in a fixed location.

But the stars would have none of it. They ambled around freely, blinking and bleating, and scrambling and jumbling all Hoshi's designs.

Hoshi crossed his arms and harrumphed. "What good are stars that don't do what they're asked?" he wondered aloud. He was just about to give up and call his father when he noticed that the stars were not really all in a jumble; they were moving in their own, orderly way.

He dropped his staff t his side. "That's it," he encouraged them, "Keep it up! Now you've got it..."

The stars moved in their own time and in their own way. And, hearing Hoshi's kind words they ordered themselves so as to create lines and shapes against the night sky.

Finally, when the night was at its darkest, Hoshi's father came to see what he had done.

"It's not a fire-breathing dragon," explained Hoshi, still trying to understand what the stars had created.

Hoshi's father smiled and shook his head. "No," he said, laying his hand on his young son's shoulder. "It is not a fire-breathing dragon. It is something much better. It is a new starherd, gently tending his stars."

Your Feedback is Priceless

Do you like the book?
It'll help us immensely if you write a couple of words.

Only your reviews allow the book to be found
and noticed among the crowd.

✎ Write a Review

This link leads directly
to the page of reviews:

https://cutt.ly/12fWkvd

Or use QR-Code:

Printed in Great Britain
by Amazon

18740566R00018